# IS IT HARD?
# IS IT EASY?

By Mary McBurney Green

Illustrations By Len Gittleman

NEW YORK: YOUNG SCOTT BOOKS

Here are four friends,
Bill, Ann, Tim, and Sue.
Let's see what each
of them can do.

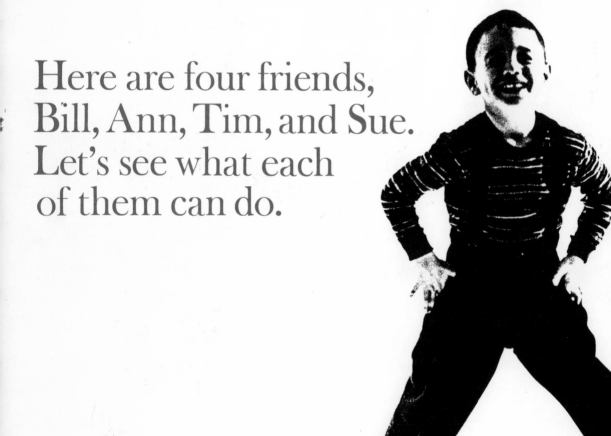

Ann skips with a skip, skip, skip.

Skipping is easy for Ann.

But Ann's friend, Sue, can't skip.

She hops instead. Skipping is hard for Sue.

But Sue can tie
her own shoes.
"Easy for me," says Sue.

When Ann tries to tie
her own shoelace,
it comes undone
and drags on the floor.
"It's hard for me," says Ann.

Look! There goes Bill,
climbing a tree from branch to branch,
almost to the top without a stop.
Tim gets stuck on a branch below.
Bill calls, "It's easy, I'll help you."

Is it hard for you to catch and throw?

Not for Tim! Look at that ball go!

Bill can throw too,
but he can't really catch.
The ball slips through his fingers
and falls to the ground.

Can you take a bath
all by yourself?
That's just what Ann can do.
She rubs and she scrubs each knee.
"That's easy for me," says Ann.

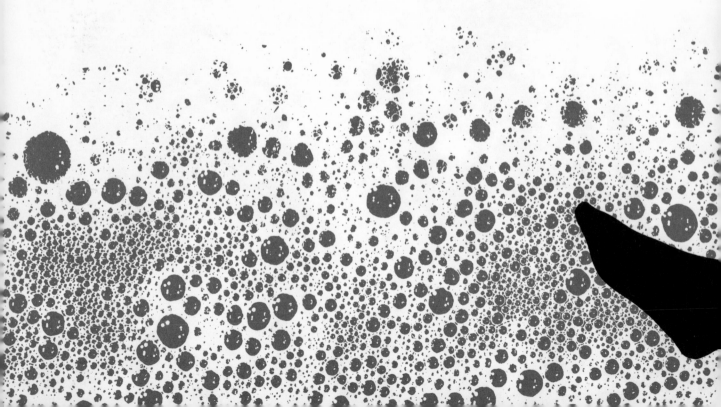

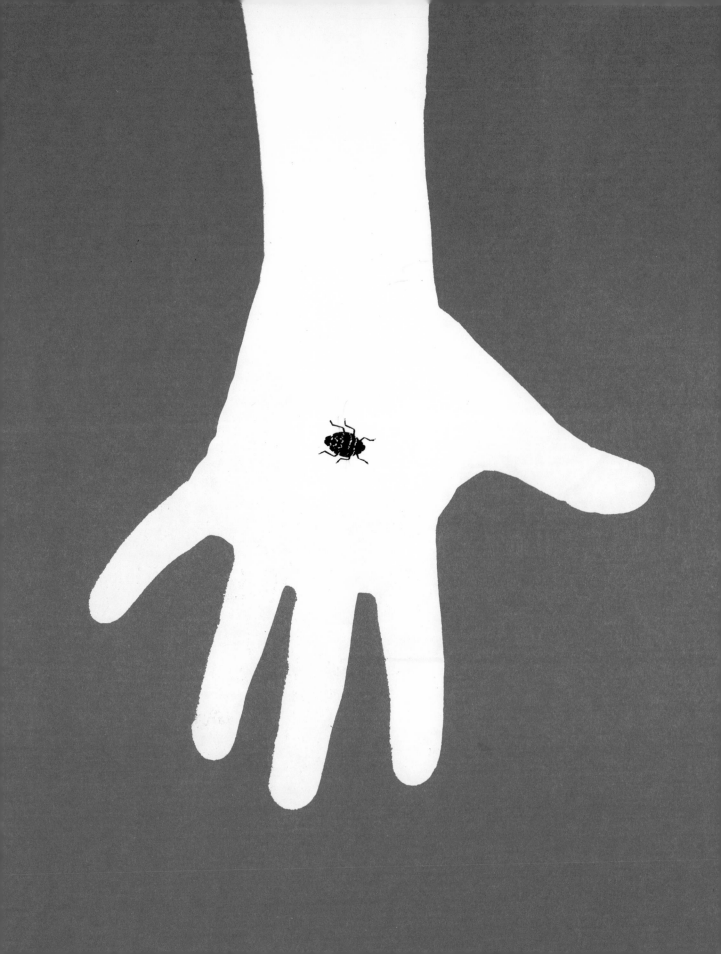

Holding worms and tickly bugs
is something that's easy for Sue to do.
She holds them right in the palm
of her hand. Ann looks on,
but she doesn't try it.
"Not today," says Ann.

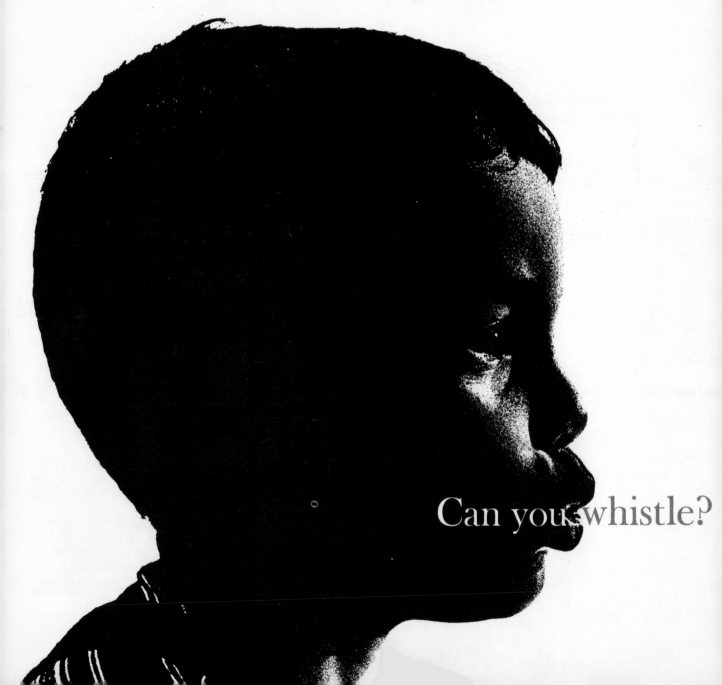

Bill can whistle.
Sharp and shrill,
he puckers his lips.
"Like this," says Bill.

Can you whistle?

"I'll soon be whistling too," says Tim.

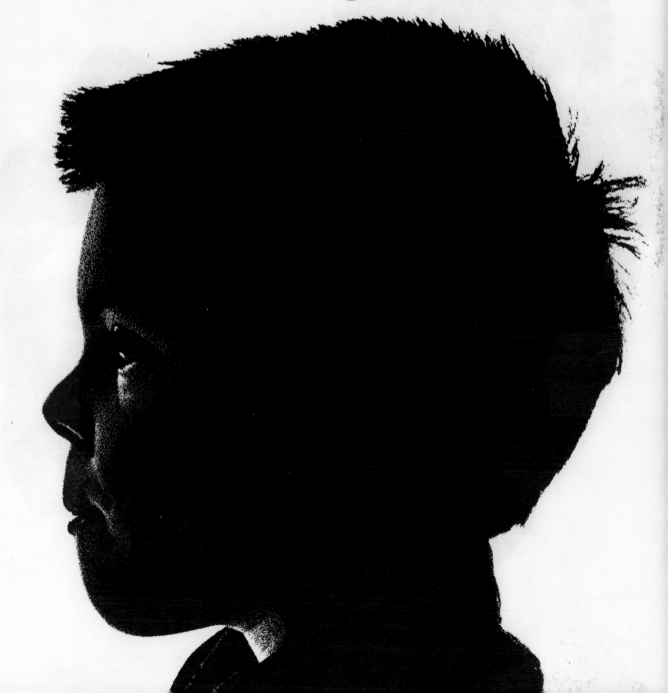

Tim knows how
to turn a somersault.
With a push from his toes,
over he goes.
Bill stops
on his head and his hands
until Tim gives him a push.

Then over Bill goes.

Bill, Ann, Tim, and Sue—
Here's something easy
they all can do.
Up in the air and down again,
it's fun on the seesaw.

There are some things that are hard for anyone to do— pounding nails so they go in straight.

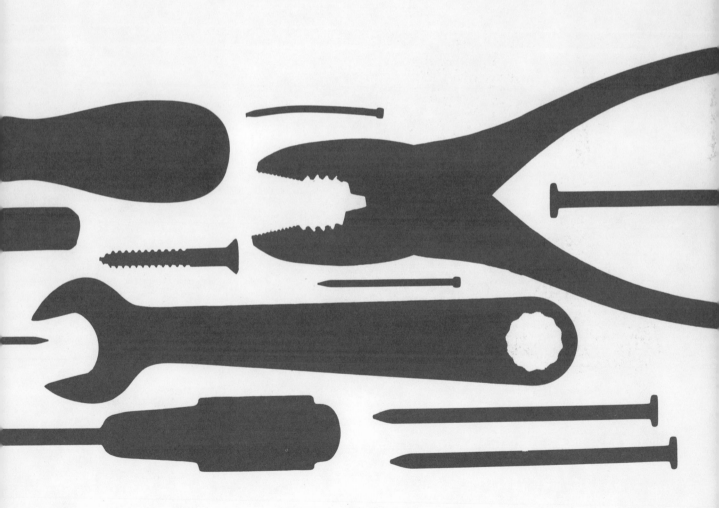

And there are some things
that are hard to do alone,
but easy to do together.

For everyone,
some things are hard
and some are easy.
The things that are easy for
you to do may be
hard for Bill or Tim
or Ann or Sue.

Now tell me about you.
What is easy
and what is hard
for you to do?

To Neal Gittleman, Lorrie Klaben,
Marc Capalbo and Eliza Brownjohn,
who played the parts of
Bill *and* Ann *and* Tim *and* Sue.